Me
+
Tree

Alexandria Giardino

Illustrated by
Anna + Elena Balbusso

Creative   Editions

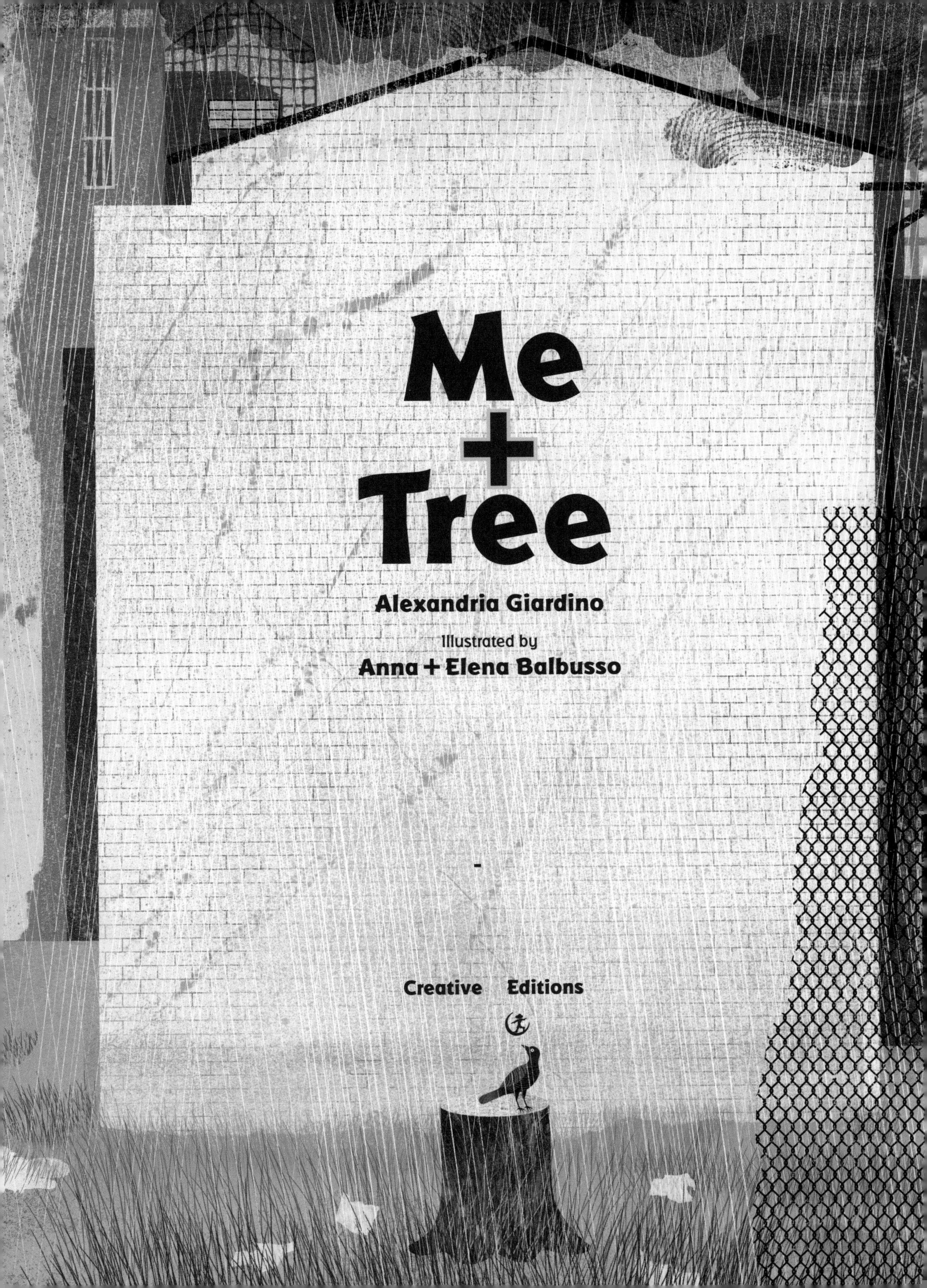

On the edge of a playground, a thick stump peeked out between weeds.

The stump had once been a tall tree with apples to eat, branches to swing from, and a trunk to climb.

But over time, people had picked all the
apples, carried off the branches, and
chopped down the trunk, and that's how
the tree became a stump.

Every now and then, someone sat on it,
but mostly no one paid any attention to it.

One day, a new girl
stood alone on the
playground. The kids
were so busy playing,
they didn't notice her.
So she looked around for
something to do, and that's
when she spotted the stump.

"Hello, old tree," she whispered, as she leaned against the stump's cool side and rested her head on its flat top. With her fingertip she followed its rings and imagined each told a chapter of the tree's story. The stump grew warm beneath her cheek.

"I have a story, too," she said. Then, slowly at first, she began to draw on the stump.

She drew a young couple planting a sapling in their budding garden.

She drew a tiny girl dancing with her family beneath a tree. The drawing was so vivid, the sound of music and laughter seemed to float on a breeze.

Her finger swirled as she drew a feast of roasted meat and a sweet apple pie, its fragrant steam spiraling upward.

Her gestures slowed as she outlined the intricate details of a house. Its wood frame, made of sturdy branches, was strong, and the house was full of love.

The girl began to scribble. Her heartbeat
raced in her fingertip.

She drew people carrying cloth suitcases
that held precious things. She drew people
waving goodbye to their gardens and their
animals. The girl's tears fell like clear ink
drops onto the stump.

She drew a boat hastily made of broken houses. She drew people crowded together, among them a girl. The spray of giant waves stung her eyes.

Then she drew skyscrapers, a playground, empty faces, and a girl and a stump that no one paid any attention to.

"I see you," she whispered.

That's when something beautiful broke
open deep within the stump, and a tiny
green shoot unfurled toward the girl.

The girl drew
a small heart
on the stump.
In it, she wrote
"Me + Tree."

Text copyright © 2020 by Alexandria Giardino

Illustrations copyright © 2020 by Anna and Elena Balbusso

Edited by Amy Novesky and Kate Riggs

Designed by Rita Marshall

Published in 2020 by Creative Editions

P.O. Box 227, Mankato, MN 56002 USA

Creative Editions is an imprint of The Creative Company

www.thecreativecompany.us

Printed in China

Library of Congress Cataloging-in-Publication Data

Names: Giardino, Alexandria, author. / Balbuso, Anna, illustrator. / Balbusso, Elena, illustrator.

Title: Me plus tree / by Alexandria Giardino; illustrated by Anna and Elena Balbusso.

Summary: A young girl and an old tree learn from each other how
to find their purpose and foster healing in the world.

Identifiers: LCCN 2019056670 / ISBN 978-1-56846-346-9

Subjects: CYAC: Trees—Fiction. / Friendship—Fiction. / Identity—Fiction.

Classification: LCC PZ7.1.G4977 Me 2021 DDC [E]—dc23

First edition 9 8 7 6 5 4 3 2 1